REDBIRD
A SOVEREIGN MOUNTAIN NOVELLA

RAYA MORRIS EDWARDS

Redbird
By Raya Morris Edwards
Copyright © 2024 Morris Edwards Publishing

FIRST EDITION

Cover Design by @designsbycharlyy
Editing by Morally Gray Editing Services

This novella is for anyone who wants to be plowed by a huge, sexy cowboy. Honestly, me too.

Xx,
Raya

AUTHOR'S NOTE

This novella is set six years after Sovereign and is intended to be read as an extended epilogue to the book. If you haven't read Sovereign, you will need to before reading this novella, or it will not make sense.

Thank you to everyone who fell in love with Gerard, Keira, and Sovereign Mountain.

Sovereign was a culmination of many things that are incredibly important to me. Of the stories I grew up reading, of the memories from the ranch where I learned to ride, and many of my personal experiences growing up in rural America. I can't thank each and every one of you who loved it enough.

A special thank you to Corinne and Lexie, who encouraged me to keep writing when I was positive there wasn't a place for a spicy, BDSM, western romance about grief, healing, and finding acceptance.

TRIGGER WARNINGS AND TAGS

Heavy pregnancy and family planning related content
Brief mentions of past trauma

SEXUAL CONTENT TAGS/WARNINGS

Explicit sexual depictions
BDSM - D/s style relationship
Somnophilia
Use of toys
Impact play
Dirty talk
Degradation & praise

CHAPTER ONE

KEIRA

SIX YEARS AFTER SOVEREIGN

At the intersection of where Sovereign Mountain once met Garrison Farms is a little valley. And walking through it, with his horse, Shadow, at his side, is my husband.

Head down, dark hat covering his face.

On Shadow is our son, holding tight to his mane. I tell my husband that our son, Cash, is too young to ride bareback and he tells me there's no holding our boy back. Gerard has a knack for horsemanship, and that talent runs through Cash's veins.

He's barely six, but he already wants to ride barefoot, no saddle or bridle. Just his fingers gripping their mane. He's a daredevil. Sometimes I wonder if things had been different for Gerard, he would have been just like Cash.

Wild and free.

I thought about that a lot at first—what might have been. Sometimes with a pang of sadness. But after six years, that sadness has faded for us both.

We're both healing, slowly, but surely. Learning to trust more every day, learning to lean into each other and forget the injustices of our pasts.

I squint, shading my eyes as I gaze at my husband and son coming over the hill. Gerard wears the same clothes he always has—a worn Henley, usually blue like his eyes, work pants, and steel toed boots.

His short, dark hair is covered by his black cowboy hat, pushed low over his eyes. He wears the same boots and pants he wore when I met him. I can tell because I've patched the inside seam a dozen times. Gerard believes in buying land and cattle—and spoiling me on occasion—but never spending on himself.

Well, except for when he paid off half of South Platte so he could run my husband over with a herd of cattle and get away with it. I'm the single most expensive thing he's ever bought just for himself.

A hot gust of wind carries the smell of spring over the front porch. I curl my toes against the floorboards.

The sight of my husband and son like this fills me with pride. It's been six years and I'm positive now that I want at least one more baby.

I haven't talked to Gerard yet, but I plan to be pregnant before the end of the year. We took a break after Cash to just enjoy having a son together. But now I feel I'm ready.

Maybe this time it'll be a girl with red hair like mine. I smile at the thought.

Cash came out a spitting image of his father. Big, blue eyes and curly dark hair. It didn't take long for him to start acting like him too. As soon as he was old enough to walk and put on a pair of boots, he was swaggering around the yard. Hands on his hips, squinting at horses and slapping cattle as they went by.

I smile, watching as they draw closer and enter the yard. Instead of heading to the barn, Gerard lifts his head and sees me waiting. He clicks his fingers for Shadow and the huge gelding turns and carries my son to the bottom of the steps.

"What are you doing, mom?" Cash asks, leaning in and resting his chin on Shadow's mane.

"Waiting for you," I say. "What are you doing?"

He straightens, pointing back at the valley. "We went up to the cliffs. Dad's showing me where he runs the cattle when he changes the pasture around."

I look past him to my husband, walking towards me with that habitually stern expression on his face. It's the face that makes me remember why I never take off the silver collar around my neck. Not once in the seven years we've been married.

His pale blue gaze flicks up and catches mine. He gives me that look— the one that always gets my panties to drop around my ankles whenever he wants. My entire body tingles, like it did when we first met.

"Careful up in the cliffs," I say lightly.

"Why?" Cash demands.

I turn to Gerard, who has his hands on his hips. He shrugs, glancing back.

"Wouldn't want to get caught between them," he says. "Not when the cattle are coming through."

Cash squints, screwing up his face as he stares over the fields. He's trying to make sense of what his father is saying, but he'll never admit there might be something in the world he can't comprehend.

"Okay," he says finally. He turns to me, ready for the next thing. "I'm hungry. What's for dinner?"

I put my hands on my hips. "I don't know, baby. What are you making?"

He looks horrified and Gerard's eyes glint. A ghost of a smile passes over his mouth.

"I can't cook, mom," Cash says.

Gerard lifts him down from Shadow and gathers the reins. "Maybe you should go help your mother, son," he says. "You're not too young to learn."

Cash wilts, stuffing his hands in his pockets. I pull him near, hugging him against my hip and ruffling his dark curls.

"We're having breakfast," I say. "It's Sunday so your dad gets to pick."

"And he always picks breakfast," Cash says, his mood improving.

Like father, like son. They'd live off biscuits and gravy if I let them. Cash takes his hat off and hits it against his thigh, the way Gerard does, to clear the dust. "Alright, let's go."

"Where you headed?" Gerard asks.

"Gotta help with Shadow," he says, like it's obvious.

I nod and Gerard hands Cash the reins. I watch them cross the yard and enter the barn, Shadow's hooves clopping on the floor. They disappear and I hear my son's voice faintly, still asking incessant questions.

My heart warms as my husband answers. Gerard has so much patience for him, just as much as he has for me.

It's everyone else in the world who pisses him off.

I pad barefoot through the front hall and into the living room. It looks exactly the same as the day he offered me a contract to be his submissive. Except, now our son's toys are strewn across the floor. There's a stack of tin cars by the hearth and pile of sticks he brought in from the yard in the fireplace.

All evidence of the life we've built together in the last seven years.

Heart warm, I head to the kitchen and start taking things from the fridge. After Cash was born, Gerard decided to designate Sunday as the one time a week where no one but our family are allowed in the ranch house. All the hired help and wranglers take a day off in their homes, in the employee housing to the west of the house.

The very last day of the week is my favorite.

For a few different reasons.

On Sunday morning, Gerard and Cash go out to do their rounds. My son insists he be involved in everything Gerard does, but my husband only has time for it on Sundays. That's when he sets our boy on the saddle in front of him and they ride out to the border. Sometimes they're back by noon. Other days they stay out, just riding the land.

"This'll be his when we retire," Gerard says sometimes. "He needs to know it like the back of his hand."

Sometimes, I take Angel and go with them. Other days, I like the quiet of the house when it's just me.

Tonight, the kitchen is too quiet so I turn on Maddie's radio. Peaceful music fills the sunny space as I roll out biscuit dough and start cutting. Maddie has all the resources in the world at her fingertips, but she still uses a chipped coffee mug to cut her biscuits. I understand—there's something about the worn porcelain that's comforting. Like hundreds of hands have done this before me and a hundred more will do it when I'm gone.

My mind drifts.

We spent the last few years resting and raising our son. We both needed to learn to be a married couple and let time heal the wounds of the past. I needed to process my first marriage and everything that had happened since I met Gerard. Our beginning was scorching hot, but with it came death, deceit, and the realization that we were both broken.

In the last six years, we've picked up all the pieces together. We've healed through our daily rituals.

Some of them are simple and sweet. Like the meals I make for him or the kisses he presses to my forehead before he leaves in the morning.

Others are so much darker, in a way that makes my toes curl just thinking about them. Pain to teach me it's safe to be vulnerable with him. Pleasure to heal me from the years of having my needs trampled on.

These rituals fuel our intimacy. At night, when the doors are closed. When the ranch sleeps.

There, I find him, intimately. In the harsh darkness when it's just our bodies, the bull skull watching over us, and the heat of leather against skin.

My body tingles, wide awake.

I hear a step in the hall, heavy like Gerard's boot. It's followed by the light patter of my son's bare feet. Cash tears down the hall and I hear him scramble up the stairs, probably heading for the shower. I know he's covered in grime, but I've got him trained to wash up before dinner, despite his frequent protests.

For a second, the house is quiet. But I know my husband is right outside. The kitchen door opens. A tingle moves up my spine and my nipples tighten under my dress.

His big, broad hands slide around my waist. My hands go still as he kisses the nape of my neck.

A hint of warmth. The tickle of his beard. The graze of his teeth.

"You smell good," he murmurs.

He turns me around abruptly, bending me back over the table. I'm in a thin sundress with a ruched bodice. When he presses up against me, my breasts spill from the neckline and the skirt rides up my thighs.

The feeling of his work clothes against my bare skin takes my breath away. Rough, creased to his hard body underneath. My lids flutter as he bends in, takes my face in his hand to turn it, and kisses my mouth. Then he pulls away and flips me around, pressing me back against the counter. The warm palm of his hand skims over my stomach and slides down the inside of my thigh.

And back up again. Stopping an inch below my pussy.

Fire floods my veins.

My head spins.

He's so good at this. He starts out gentle, then gives me just a trace of his tongue. He holds back until I'm begging for it. Then he kisses me like he's starving, only tearing his mouth from mine to drag it over my neck.

He kisses my cleavage and my hands, covered in flour, dig into his shirt. This isn't the first time he's interrupted me in the kitchen and left with dusty white handprints all over his body.

"You're so pretty," he says distractedly. "My beautiful redbird."

Heat radiates from my face. "You'd better stop distracting me if you want dinner."

He glances up. "You can take a break while Cash washes up."

Before I can speak, he picks me up and wraps my legs around his waist. I grip his shoulders as he carries me around the corner and into the walk-in pantry.

The door slams and he crushes me against the wall.

Kisses burn down my throat. His teeth graze my breasts. My head falls back as his rough fingers slip between my legs. Instead of stopping this time, he cups my pussy in his rough hand. Making it pulse under the pressure.

"Good girl," he says. "You did good, keeping your pussy bare for me to use."

He didn't lay out panties this morning, just a bra, so that's all I have on under my dress. It gives me such a thrill when he praises me for obeying him. My toes curl as his touch slips over my sex and out from below my skirt so he can rub himself against me.

I can feel him, big and hard, under his work pants.

My hips rise of their own accord, up against the enormous ridge. I can already tell my pussy is drenched, as it always is for him. All it takes is the darkness of his voice, like thunder over the mountains. The brush of his hand, so rough, but so gentle for me.

And I'm at his mercy.

His hand slides up the back of my neck and gathers my hair, wrapping it twice around his fist. My breath catches as he drags my head back. Forcing me to look into his impassive, blue stare.

Then he reaches between our bodies and his zipper hisses. My eyes flutter as he unleashes his cock and the head hits against my clit. Without prep or ceremony, he wraps his hand around the base and guides his heavy length into my pussy.

Inch by inch.

I groan softly, trying to rotate my hips to fit him. That familiar burn starts and my body responds like wildfire. Aching and trying to thrust against him. He's written himself into my veins and my body wants nothing but him. Nothing but his taste, his scent, the weight and fullness of his cock deep inside me.

I gasp as he settles up against my cervix. At this angle, he can't get in all the way, but that doesn't stop him from trying.

Our eyes lock and I whimper. He brushes my hair back from my face.

"I think you can take it, redbird," he says gruffly. "You've been a good whore for me, you can do it again."

My nails rake over his shoulders and neck. Leaving flour all over him.

"Please," I gasp. "Please, sir."

He tilts his head, drawing his cock out slowly.

"Please...what?" he says.

11

My teeth bite down hard on my lower lip and release it, leaving the tender skin tingling.

"Please fuck me, sir," I whisper.

His hips go still and his hand releases my hair. My breath catches as he slides a finger under my discreet collar, pulling it tight. I'm so turned on I can't control the way my pussy grips him.

"Mine," he says. "Say it."

"Yours," I breathe. "Sir."

He releases the collar and braces his hand on the wall beside me. Upstairs, I can hear the water running through the pipes. We have a few more minutes to ourselves before we have to go back to being parents.

He draws out, dragging his cock to the head. Then he slams it back into me and my nails pierce his skin. My vision flashes and I hear how wet I am.

"Fuck me, redbird, you're tight," he groans.

Sweat breaks out on my upper back. I'm flat against the wall as he starts fucking hard, giving me all the power in that broad body. My skirt is up around my waist and my hair is tangled around my sweaty neck. His other hand grips my thigh, holding me up easily and spreading me open at the same time.

He slams me into the wall, taking what he wants. My pleasure sparks and gets closer every time the head of his cock drags over my G-spot.

He pushes to the hilt, until it hurts, and grinds into my clit. Then I break, hot pleasure bursting through me. I shake, pumping around him, whimpering through my teeth.

He groans and somehow goes even harder. My spine arcs, desperately trying to make room. This time, it's too much.

A whimper pushes past my lips and he eases up on me. My pussy is so full I swear I can feel him past my navel. Gently stroking my cervix with the head of his cock. I'm not used to taking him at this angle, usually I'm on my back to make more room.

His mouth brushes over mine. His body stiffens.

Then he comes, hips slamming into me as the pleasure washes over him. I feel the warmth deep inside. His groan turns into a heavy growl deep in his chest. He buries his face in my neck.

Our bodies go still.

Lungs and hearts pumping.

He lifts his head, brushing his lips over my forehead. My heart melts.

How is he so rough and so gentle all at once?

The water turns off upstairs. He pulls his cock from me and zips himself up in one movement. Then he leaves the pantry and returns in a moment with a cool, wet cloth. He sinks down on his knees and parts my thighs, cleaning our arousal and cum from my body.

He kisses my clit. And I'm a puddle on the floor.

"I guess I should make biscuits," I say, stumbling over my words.

The corner of his mouth turns up. "I guess so."

My face is so sweaty and flushed I can't hide it as I wash my hands and go back to laying out the biscuits. He leaves and takes his overwhelming presence with him, heading upstairs.

In a few moments, I hear Cash talking with him. I press the back of my hands to my cheek. I need some iced tea after that.

By the time I hear them climbing down the stairs, I'm cooled down. There are pitchers of iced tea and lemonade ready on the table. The biscuits are in the oven and sausages crackle on the stove. My face isn't flushed anymore and my hair is smoothed back.

"Dinner smells good," Cash says, popping up behind me. "Smells like biscuits."

"Well, you know I don't serve breakfast without biscuits," I say, lifting him up to sit on the counter. He watches as I pour a glass of lemonade and hand it to him. He drinks, testing it experimentally. Just one time, when he was three, I gave him lemonade that wasn't sweet enough and, I swear, he'll remember it forever.

"It's good," he says.

"Cash," Gerard says, walking into the kitchen in just his t-shirt and pants, a towel in hand. "Say thank you to your mother when she serves you."

"Thank you, mom," he says, looking guilty. "Sorry, I forgot."

I kiss his head. "You're welcome, baby."

I give Gerard a glance over my shoulder and he gives me a glance back. It's a silent exchange of me telling him he's too stern with Cash and him

13

telling me that he knows what he's doing. For a second, I consider pushing back, but then I remember that Gerard shows his love differently than I do and that's alright.

"Can we eat on the porch?" Cash says, dropping to the ground.

"Sure," I say. "Why don't you go set the table?"

He nods and starts gathering up the utensils and napkins. He's not very good at it, I always have to do some subtle corrections. But I'm over the moon that he wants to help.

He heads out, everything in a bundle held to his chest. Gerard leans on the counter and gives me a look. Heat creeps up my neck and I pretend to ignore him as I flip the sausages.

But it's so hard to ignore the way those pale eyes follow my every move. Finally, I turn.

"What?" I ask, not unkindly.

"Nothing," he says. "I just have a good looking wife."

I bite my lip, ducking my head. Never sure how to react when he looks at me like that. I give him everything. My body, my mind. There are no secrets, nothing between us anymore. And yet, he's so hungry for more.

It's thrilling, overwhelming.

At least, we'll never get bored together.

We eat on the porch as the sun sets over the mountains. The grass in the fields is already high and it moves in waves. In the distance, I hear the cattle settling down. It's a sound so familiar it brings me peace every night.

Cash plays in the yard for a while. Around eight, Gerard sends him up to brush his teeth and go to bed. When I'm finished with cleaning the kitchen, I sneak up the stairs and peer into his room.

My little boy is curled up, head on the pillow. Eyes hazy and fixed out his window.

"Goodnight, baby," I whisper.

He glances over his shoulder, smile sleepy. Then he's out, snoring as the moon rises and casts a pale blue glow over his bed. Heart overflowing, I close his door and go back downstairs to find my husband.

CHAPTER TWO

GERARD

I watch her step onto the porch. The moon is so bright tonight it almost feels like day. Everything glows midnight blue.

Her hips sway as she descends the steps. She's in that little, blue printed sundress that makes my heart pound. It falls off her shoulder and the fabric is tight over her breasts. The soft swell of her cleavage spills over beautifully.

Her eyes dart up in a coy glance. She knows what she does to me.

My dick twitches in my pants. It's Sunday night and I'll make her pay for teasing me later.

I stand in the yard, waiting. She draws up beside me, her bare feet noiseless, and I take her by the throat to kiss her mouth.

God, she tastes like heaven. A little bit of sweetness still on her tongue. I lick it off and kiss up the side of her neck. Her head falls back, spilling brilliant red down her back.

She's breathing heavily when I let her go. Her fingers dig into my arms.

"It's Sunday night," I say.

Her throat bobs and her lashes flutter down. Pink blossoms over her cheeks and cleavage. "I know."

I pull her soft body against mine. My lips rest on her hair, breathing in that familiar scent. "Let's take a ride first."

"Where?"

"Anywhere," I say. "It's bright out, and cool for once."

She nods and I use my head to push hers to the side, pressing my mouth to her throat. Her hand comes up, digging into my shirtfront. Between our bodies, fire crackles. She moans and rubs her hips against my thigh.

I'm hard, I want her again, but I can hold back.

For now.

I take her hand and lead the way to the barn. Shadow is still awake, his head hanging over the gate. On the other side, Angel is already asleep. The stall beside her houses Angel's son, Starlight.

He wasn't broken until a year ago. To my surprise, he was the easiest horse I've ever trained. He took to it like a fish to water. Within eight months, I felt comfortable letting Keira up on him.

"Angel's asleep," she whispers. "I don't want to wake her."

I smile. She's so sweet with how deeply she cares for the animals.

"Take Starlight," I say. "You can ride him bareback."

She nods, tiptoeing around to open his door. I open Shadow's stall and click my tongue and he walks out so I can slip his bridle on. Without the stirrups, Keira can't get up on Starlight, so I help her mount up. Then I swing my leg over Shadow and we head out.

We ride quietly through the yard. I glance at her, soaking in the sight of my wife as she should be. Her soft, freckled thighs are bare, her skirt hitched up.

She's free, beautiful, and mine.

I have never loved anything so deeply as I love this woman. It started small, like a controlled burn. Her heat and sweetness ate up all the dead parts of me, leaving me charred, but ready for new growth. Now she's the most peaceful wildfire I've ever known.

"Do you want to run?" she asks.

"Starlight can't keep up with Shadow," I say.

16

She clicks her tongue and Starlight shifts into a trot, then a canter, and finally a smooth gallop. For a second like a picture burned into my brain. I see her hair whip as she looks over her shoulder, flashing a smile.

"Come get me," she calls.

I shift my weight and Shadow thunders after her. Starlight is smaller, but he puts up a chase. Our horses tear over the field, making a wide circle to move through the place where the Garrison land once touched my ranch. We head down until we cross the road and enter the new plot I purchased after our marriage.

I've worked this land in the last six years. The grass is green now, the stream is dammed into a small pond. In the fall when the upper fields are dry, I'll rotate most of the cattle through here.

She pulls to a halt and I do the same, dismounting. Shadow shakes his mane and wanders off to graze. He knows enough now to give us privacy. I reach up and she lets me grip her waist, her hands going to my shoulders as I lift her to the ground. Starlight makes himself scarce.

I take her in my arms and lay her out on the grass. On her back with her skirt falling up to flash her naked thighs. Our mouths meet, and every color of the sky and mountains and the valleys in between, flashes through my body. Like the northern lights lie on her tongue.

We break apart. I brush her hair back gently.

Her eyes glitter, deep blue made black by the moonlight.

"I want another baby," she whispers.

Her words don't surprise me. The other day when I got in from chores, I found her in Cash's old nursery, folding blankets in the closet. All the baby things are already packed away. She didn't have any reason to be there, but she was. When she heard me, she mumbled something about having lost something and hurried out.

I see the way she watches Cash grow up. Proud, but with a little ache like she might cry.

Bending, I press my lips to her forehead.

"You want a baby, redbird, let's have one," I tell her.

Her eyes light up. "Really?"

"Really."

She bites her lip and then she smiles. It's breathtaking and I'm lost in it.

17

"When?" she asks eagerly.

"Anytime."

She laughs, like she's excited and nervous all at once. Her lashes glitter wet. I trace the palm of my hand down between her breasts and rest it on her lower belly. Before Cash was born, I put that little wooden foal on her stomach and dreamed of what our lives could be with a child in them.

Now I know how good it is. Sometimes it's hard, but, God, it's so fucking good.

"What do you want?" she asks.

"Hmm, girl this time," I say. "But whatever it is, that's fine."

She nods. "I'd like a little girl."

I wonder what a daughter of mine would be like. Cash is a carbon copy of me and I know how to manage that. I'll raise him to work the ranch and he'll fit into my world like a puzzle piece. But I know being a woman is harder, it's more dangerous. Keira is proof of that.

The notion that my daughter might suffer sparks an ugly rage in me. If she's like Keira, she'll be too sweet for this world.

For tonight, I tamp my worries down. First we'll have joy, then we can navigate the rougher waters.

So I turn my mind off and kiss her because the world is quiet tonight.

CHAPTER THREE

KEIRA

Part of me knew he'd be happy to start trying again. But when he says yes right away, I can't keep the tears back. One slips into my hair. His thumb comes up and brushes it away.

"Are you happy?" he asks.

I just nod.

"Good," he says. "That's all I want, redbird."

At first, it was hard for me to believe that was truly all he wanted. I spent so much time with my first husband who didn't care what I needed. It frightened me at first that Gerard was ready and willing to give me anything. It took me a long time to realize his kindness isn't a trap. Or a trick so he can hurt me, the way it was with Clint.

But old habits die hard. Even now, it makes my head spin that there's no cruelty hidden under his actions.

When he says he loves me, he means it.

When he does something for me, there's no catch.

I clear my throat. "Kiss me again," I beg.

He does, giving me a taste of his tongue before pulling back. His mouth is firm and warm on my neck as he kisses down to my collarbone. I feel the brush of his palm over my breast. Then he tugs and cool air washes over my right breast and nipple, tightening it.

My eyes flutter shut. The cool air is replaced by his hot mouth.

My spine arcs, my hips strain up.

He presses them back down, his palm right above my clit. "Stay still, redbird," he orders.

"Yes, sir," I gasp.

He lowers his mouth back to my nipple, curling it with the tip of his tongue. He flicks it and I moan. Then he sucks it with gentle pulses.

Heat flares between my thighs. I'm acutely aware of the emptiness like a heartbeat inside me.

I need him.

I need my husband.

I need my Sovereign.

I need him to take me here on the soft earth. Then bring me back to the house when he's done, my palms and knees stained green. I want to fall asleep satisfied, with brambles in my hair and starlight burned into my eyes.

My knees spread. The heel of his palm slips lower to feel where I'm still wet from the last time he took me.

He strokes my pussy gently. My chest heaves. Overhead, the stars and moon are bright and blurry through my lashes.

The wanting is so strong it's like a gravitational pull. I would say like the tide, but it never ebbs. It only flows and then flows stronger until it pulls me under.

Until I drown in him.

Without warning, he flips onto his back and drags me across his broad body to straddle his hips. My hair falls back, my fingers dig into his shirt. Between my thighs, I feel his raw power.

Desperate, I press my naked, wet pussy against the hardness under his pants and grind.

But he stops me. Big hands on my thighs, keeping them down. Our eyes lock and I have to bite back a whine. I know better than to protest.

For a moment, I see a flash of cruelty in his eyes and I have to remind myself that this is just play.

At the end of it, his hands will be gentle.

"I think you should wait," he says, his voice low in his chest. "Show me how good you can be for me."

Desire shivers down my thighs and makes my toes curl in the dewy grass. He takes me by the neck with his rough palm, pulling me down. Until our mouths are inches apart.

"I think you need spanked first," he says. "Just to remind you of your place. Then I'll fuck your cunt, you needy, little whore."

Oh God, he knows exactly what to say. He always has, but after six years together, he can bring me to my knees with a few short words.

His eyes soften.

"But for right now, just be with me," he says softly. "Wife."

I melt into him, laying my head on his broad chest. His heart is a steady drum, and in it I feel my world. I swear sometimes his blood flows like the river, his heart beats like the rain coming over the mountains, and his skin burns like the summer sun.

He's lived so long on Sovereign Mountain that they are one and the same.

Perhaps that's why I fell so hard. He'd brought me here and showed me what he loved first. I saw the care he took of it and deep down knew he would love me the same way.

"What's going on in this head?" he asks quietly.

His fingertips brush my hair, playing with the strands.

"Are you sure you want another baby?" I whisper.

"You sound worried. Are you already pregnant?"

"No," I say quickly. "I'm still taking my birth control. I just want us both to be sure before we start trying."

He rumbles in his chest, like he's pleased. His palm rests on my back.

"Do *you* want another baby?" he asks.

I nod, chewing on my lip. His other hand comes up and cradles my thigh, holding my body over his. I love laying on him like this and soaking in the warmth of his body. He's always so calm and I feel it seep through and slow my heart.

"Let's make another baby then," he says. "I meant it when I said yes."

My stomach swoops and I push myself up to rest my chin on his chest. He's gazing up at the stars, their pale light in his eyes.

"Just like that?" I whisper.

He glances down and a smile ghosts over his mouth. "Just like that."

I can't hold back my laughter. It's pure joy and it bubbles up in me. Overflowing. God, that feels so good.

"I love you," I whisper.

He gives me that look—the one that's pure longing and admiration all at once. The first time I noticed it was when I caught him staring at me in the cabin, all those years ago. When I'd asked him what he was looking at and he said, "Just you."

He says that a lot. I'll catch him staring and it's not for any reason. He's just looking. One time I pushed him for a real answer and he took off his hat and slapped my ass with it.

"I'm just looking at what belongs to me, redbird," he said.

I drag myself back to the present, knowing I'm going to have my fill of my husband later tonight.

"Did you take your pill today?" he asks.

I shake my head. "I thought maybe you'd say yes."

He rumbles, a quiet laugh. "You've turned into a woman who knows what she wants."

"I just know you."

"You know me and you know what you want," he muses.

I'm getting uncomfortable with being in his spotlight. "What do you think Cash will think about being a brother?"

His jaw works. "It depends. I think he'll like it overall."

I furrow my brow. "I hope we don't have adjustment problems."

"There will always be problems," he says. "We'll figure them out."

I nod, tracing my finger over the buttons of his Henley. Enjoying how firm his chest is, how it feels like a warm slab under my touch. It was one of the first things I noticed when he fucked me the night he saved me from the fire—how big and broad and warm he was against my body.

"What do you think it will be?" I muse.

"Maybe a little, redheaded girl. It'd be nice to get a child with your sweetness, redbird."

"Cash is sweet," I scold. "At least, when he chooses to be."

"He's bullheaded," he says. "I've got my eye on him."

"What if we get a redheaded girl who's just like you?"

"That's a deadly combination. I don't know what I'd do."

I love it when he's relaxed and I can hear the amusement like a current beneath his voice. It used to be such a rare thing to see his humanity.

Now, I see it flashing here and there, like the sun darting from behind the clouds. When we married, I thought I loved Sovereign as deeply as I could. But watching him be a father to my son has made me realize it's possible to love him more deeply still.

CHAPTER FOUR

GERARD

She's sweet and flustered as we put the horses away. She always is Sunday nights—she knows what happens when I get her up to our room. I watch her from the corner of my eye. Noting the flush of her cheeks and the way she works her lower lip with her teeth.

The way she looks everywhere, but at me.

I send her inside and finish locking up the barn. When I'm done, I move slowly through the house and lock the windows and doors. Mostly to give her time to get ready for me.

Then, I head upstairs.

The door to our bedroom is ajar. On the far, opposite side of the hall is Cash's room. The house has thick walls and noise doesn't travel from one side to the other. Still, I make sure to shut our door and lock it firmly.

My breath catches as my eyes fall on my wife. She's on her knees at the end of the bed.

Beautiful, curvy body in a little, lace thing. The kind I have to work not to tear with the calluses on my palms. My leather collar sits around her neck, her red hair spilling over her back and shoulders. Her palms are open and laid out on her thighs and her eyes are lowered.

I go to her and rest my fingertips on the top of her head. She keeps still while I stroke her hair. Then I tap her head twice and she releases her perfect posture, leaning into my leg. Trustingly, she rubs her cheek against my thigh.

"You stay here while I shower, redbird," I tell her.

"Yes, sir."

This is the part she loves most. The waiting. The anticipation of knowing what's coming, but not when. The part that gets her so wet it leaves glittering arousal on the floor between her knees.

I take my time. Instead of putting on my sweats, I opt for my good pants and shirt. She loves it when I punish her while still fully dressed.

I push the bathroom door open and lean in the doorway. Her head stays down.

"How were you this week?"

She bites her lip, working it. "I think...good, sir."

"You think? Either you were or you weren't."

She squirms. "I was."

I cross the room and take the leather strip with the implements inside from the dresser. We've added a few things here and there, namely a riding crop that she loves. It cracks like a gunshot, but never breaks her delicate skin. It only leaves little pink marks over her soft, round ass and thighs.

A quiver moves through her when I touch the looped end between her breasts. And drag it up to her chin and use it to lift her eyes to mine.

They're wide and deep blue. So sweet.

"Where do you want it, redbird?" I ask.

She gasps as the looped end trails back down her neck. Over her stomach and between her thighs. I trace the wet seam of her pussy, back and forth.

"Focus," I say.

"Um, in the chair," she whispers. "Sir."

"Good girl," I praise. "How?"

Her tongue darts out to wet her mouth. "Over your lap, sir."

Her cheeks are rosy pink. Her eyes glitter like she's burning with fever. I trail the crop over her clit, making close circles. Her hips quiver and I know how badly she wants to grind up against the leather.

But she won't without permission. She's too well trained for that.

I flick my wrist. The whip cracks over the entrance of her pussy and she cries out softly as it stings her sensitive sex. Her hands clench and fall open again. Fingertips quivering.

"Let's talk," I say.

She swallows. This is the part she struggles with most. I sit in my leather armchair in the far corner. The crop goes on the table beside me and I spread my knees, giving her enough space to kneel between them.

"Unhook your collar," I say. "Crawl to me."

She obeys, shaking fingers disconnecting the leash. Then she leans down onto her hands and knees, big eyes fixed on me, and moves across the bedroom floor. Round ass and perfect hips swaying.

I point at the ground. She settles herself between my knees and lays her cheek against my thigh.

"Talk to me," I say.

Her lids flutter when I stroke through her hair and I see her focus waver. This is the part *I* love most—watching her struggle to be patient and obey when all she wants is to be filled. She's so ready to be fucked, but we have to move through each step before our ritual is complete.

It's an exercise in denial for us both.

"What do I say?" she murmurs.

"How did you feel about this week?" I press. "Just about the parts between us."

She sighs. "I loved it, sir."

"That's all."

She nods. "You know me before I even know myself."

I tilt her chin up and her eyes are hazy. "And you feel safe?"

"Yes, sir."

"What about the other night?"

I see her mind flit back. The other night, I was out late checking the fences. When I returned, she was already asleep. Curled up on her side of the bed, nothing showing but her red hair. I pulled the covers back and it

26

hit me that this was my wife. The way it sometimes does when she's doing ordinary things.

Suddenly I saw every inch of her in detail. Her soft, curvy body. The delicate marks across her lower stomach from her pregnancy. Narrow waist, full hips and thighs.

She's so soft and sweet.

My *wife*. My *woman*.

And it roused a feral part of me I couldn't hold back.

She woke with a gasp as I sank between her thighs and into her soft pussy. Not giving her time to adjust, forcing her to take the pleasure and pain all at once, like a shot of neat whiskey. She gave in, because of course she did. And I fucked her like it was the first time we touched all over again.

Bed striking the wall. Floor shaking.

Leaving us battered and bruised when the storm was over.

I pull myself back from that memory. She's blushing, pressing her forehead into my thigh to hide her face.

"Answer me, redbird," I order.

She drags her eyes up to mine, big and glittering in the low light. "Yes, sir, even the other night I felt safe."

I lift her onto my lap, parting her thighs. "Good, is there anything else?"

She shakes her head. "No, this week was good."

It was, but I still have to check in with her and give her a safe place to speak up. It's my responsibility as her Dom to ensure she feels heard.

Now that I know she does, we can move on. We won't review her behavior tonight. I correct her instantly when she steps out of line so she never has to wait and suffer unnecessarily.

Tonight is for pleasure. To remind us where we stand with each other.

"Get up," I tell her.

She obeys, climbing off my lap.

"Clothes off."

She does as she's told, stripping until her slip and panties are in her hands. I jerk my head to the chair and she goes, folding her things neatly and setting them aside. Her eyes dart up, glittering with sweet shame.

I beckon her to me.

27

This is when her steps lag. When she knows what comes next, and no matter how many times we've done this, it still gives her a thrill of fear.

I know that soft paradise between her thighs is soaked.

I lean back, spreading my knees. Her hands twist together as she approaches. She's flushed and flustered and I like seeing her broken down. I like shattering her, tasting her vulnerability.

And I love putting her back together when we're done.

"Over my knee, redbird," I say.

She obeys, draping her breathtaking body across my lap. Her ass is soft and my fingers dig into the curves of it. Running over and over the swells to bring the blood to the surface and get it moving.

My cock thrums, so hard it hurts, pushing up against her belly.

"This isn't because you've done anything wrong," I say. "This is to remind you of what you are to me, redbird."

"I understand, sir," she gasps.

"And who I am to you."

"Yes, sir."

I strike her lightly first, leaving fingerprints where her thigh meets her ass. She keeps quiet. I spank her again, harder. Then I push her right thigh to the side until it's slightly cocked so it spreads and exposes her swollen pussy.

It's flushed pink and slick with arousal. It always is after we've moved through our rituals. Her body knows what comes next and it's ready for me.

Using my finger and thumb, I spread her sex open. She quivers as I dip my fingertip inside to check how wet she is, so I can compare when I'm done.

"Clench," I order.

She obeys, the muscles of her pussy tightening and loosening. I withdraw and put my finger to my lips. Sometimes I swear I can taste her lust, laced like a drug through her wet arousal.

A tremor moves down her thigh. She's having trouble waiting.

Taking mercy on her, I spank her lightly twice. Both sides so I can watch her skin redden at the same time. After moving through so many Sunday nights with her, I've started noticing the tiny details.

The seconds between her breaths.

The difference between a tremor of anticipation and a tremor of impending orgasm.

The white of her knuckles when she feels pain versus pleasure.

There are so many shades to my redbird. And they all spill out, bringing life to my world in and out of our bedroom.

She moans and I spank her again, this time harder. Her lungs heave, but she keeps still. She's been trained for this and she knows my expectations.

I feel a ripple of resistance and I spank her again, hard enough to send vibrations deep into her core. Then twice more, until she whimpers. The resistance breaks down and she eases into me, soft body going softer still.

I love this moment.

She shudders and lets out a little sob. Her tears are silent, but I feel them fall on my arm and thigh. She can safeword me if she wants, but she won't. The euphoric high she gets from crying in the safety of my arms is too great.

Gently, I slide my other arm under her body, down between her breasts. Easing it between our bodies until I find her clit. Her hips jump at the contact. I know my fingers are rough, but she's wet and she can take it.

"Moan for me, redbird," I urge.

She whimpers, her breaths quick and close. My hand comes down on her ass, right where it meets her thigh. Right where she's so sensitive.

I glance down. Her bare feet are braced on the floor.

Then one lifts, toes curling.

She's going to come.

Quick as a flash, I stop everything and she wails in protest, devastated. I flip her in my arms so she's on her knees in my lap and brush her hair back. Her breasts heave, her nipples hard and flushed.

"What did I do wrong?" she gasps.

I shake my head. "Nothing. You're perfect. But you have to wait until I let you finish. And you know that."

She bites her lip. I take her chin in my fingers and lift her face up.

"You know that, don't you, redbird?"

She nods, knowing better than to protest. I move my hand from her face to her throat and kiss her mouth, tasting the salt of her tears. Her hips grind, mindlessly. With my mouth on hers, I reach over to the table at my side and flip the lid of the box we keep there. She tenses as I take out a little bottle and rub lube over her asshole.

A moan works its way up. I reach back into the box.

I feel the smooth, cool metal of the plug. My hand slides from her throat and down to her waist to keep her still. My other hand takes the little plug and runs it from her clit to her asshole. Gathering her silky wetness.

She breaks from my mouth, eyes glazed and breasts heaving. I press the metal tip against her flesh and she moans, her head falling back. The first time we did this, she clenched. But now she stays relaxed and her body takes it as I slip the cool metal into her ass. Fitting it in place.

She twists. Lips parting, hair falling over her breasts.

"Good fucking girl," I pant.

She pushes her face into my chest. Shuddering.

"What do you say?"

"Thank you, sir." Her voice is muffled.

I lift her in my arms and spill her out onto the bed. On her knees, facing the headboard. Her brilliant hair tumbles down her back. Her round ass is flushed pink, her thighs are marked with little stripes from the crop.

I start unbuttoning my shirt. We're so close to breaking. I need the sweet rush of her release, to taste her tears on her mouth.

There's nothing like fucking her when her walls are down.

CHAPTER FIVE

KEIRA

He presses my thighs apart and I lift my spine, offering my pussy to him. But he doesn't push into me. Instead he lowers his head, shifting down, until he's between my legs.

Trembling, I shut my eyes, overwhelmed and wanting to focus on one thing at a time.

For a second, there's nothing.

Then his tongue slides hot through my sex. The roughness of his beard rasps over my inner thighs. My nipples tighten. He loves the taste, I know by the soft growl in his chest as his tongue delves inside. He takes his time licking my pussy clean before pulling back.

I hear his step and know he's standing behind me. There's a sharp crack of pain and I yelp, spine bending as I resist the urge to look back. He's using the crop again. My pussy clenches, and with it, I tighten around the plug. Pleasure throbs and I fight it back as my inner muscles tighten.

I can't come without his permission.

Everything in me focuses on breathing the pleasure back. The looped end of the crop stings the right side of my ass. My fingers dig into the sheets. I hear a faint rip as the fabric gives way beneath my nails.

The crop strikes the backs of my thighs.

Again.

And again.

Until I sink onto my elbows and push my face into the bed. Tears soak the sheets. All the stress of the week spills over and flows out. When he hears my first sob, the crop clatters to the ground.

His body slides over mine. He lifts my head back, hand cupping my throat.

"Do you need to safeword me, redbird?" His voice is hoarse.

"No, sir," I gasp. "I need you, inside me. Please."

I can feel the ridge of his arousal, pressing against my ass. He's so hard he's twitching and I'm so wet it's dripping on the bed.

"Beg," he orders.

"Please, sir," I pant. "Please, fuck me."

I have no shame, not with him. My head is a dreamy, relaxed space and only he has the power to control what I feel.

His zipper hisses. I hear him spit into his hand and jerk his cock. His breath comes heavy and my pussy flutters with anticipation.

"Redbird," he says, voice low. "Turn around and suck my cock."

I scramble into position and he takes me by the hair and guides my face against his groin. My lips part and the thick head slips in.

Hard, hot, and far too big to fit properly.

My jaw loosens and I fall into the headspace where I can breathe through it. But he doesn't thrust.

"Lick me, redbird," he says. "I want to see you choke on it."

I'm soaked from being spanked and relaxed from crying. There's nothing in me but the driving need to do anything he asks. He fills my mouth, making my jaw ache. I push my tongue forward, trying to lick him in the little space I have.

He hums, stroking the back of my head. "Good girl, do what you can."

I force another inch in. Saliva slips down my chin as I gag, but I don't stop licking him. The feeling of his cock throbbing against my tongue is too addicting. Finally, his fist tightens in my hair and he pulls me off, a strand of wetness connecting my lips to his cock.

"What do you say?" His face is stone, eyes serious.

"Thank you for letting me suck your cock, sir." My voice is a husky whisper.

He wipes my mouth with his palm. "Good girl, now turn around and put your face in the bed. Ass up, pussy spread."

My heart thumps like a drum. He releases me and I do as he says, spreading my knees and laying my cheek against the bed.

Back arched, soaked pussy bared.

He taps the plug and turns it once. I shudder, deep in my core. Then I hear him spit again and his big fingers work the wetness over my sex.

"You're soaked," he rumbles.

"Yes, sir," I moan, eyes rolling as his middle finger slips back in for a second.

The bed dips as he kneels over me. We're in the same exact place we were the first night we fucked, except this time I'm face down, ass up. My thighs quiver as the thick, blunt head of his cock pushes against my pussy.

I gasp, unable to help myself.

The truth is, it always hurts going in. Even after all this time. He's a big man, every part of him, and I can only take him when I'm soaked.

Even then, there's always an adjustment period.

A flash of pain, an ebb of discomfort. Then he stretches me, and pleasure sparks. Drowning everything else out. He inches into me and I gasp, the pressure intense. It's so much harder to take him when I'm wearing a plug.

My muscles clench around his veined length and he groans, falling over me. Lean stomach and big, warm body against mine. He's not in all the way—he's waiting to give me the rest. Giving me time to get used to the feeling.

"How is it, redbird?" he breathes.

"Good, sir," I pant. "I'm...very full."

He slides a hand up over my stomach, between my breasts, and grips my throat. Holding me steady as his hips start pumping. Pushing me little by little to take the rest of his cock.

"Please," I whimper.

"Hush, you can take it," he says.

I know I can, and if I can't, I always have my safeword. But I don't want him to stop, I want to be forced to take the rest. I want his body on mine, his strong hands guiding me until we're fully joined.

Desperate, I push back against him. His hand slides between us and keeps me from taking the rest.

"Beg," he whispers, his voice harsh and dark. "This time, I want you to mean it."

"Please, sir," I gasp. "Please, give me your cock. I'll do anything."

He slides in a little more. I'm so desperate and so deep in a submissive state, I really would do anything for him. His grip on my throat increases. In slow, building pulses.

"I'm begging you, sir," I manage, my voice strangled.

All at once, he slides his cock to the hilt, until his body is fully against mine. A whimper works its way out. My pussy grips him, making my brain buzz with satisfaction.

He pumps his hips lightly, breaking me in until the pain ebbs.

"Good girl," he rasps, leaning forward. He flips the headboard, revealing the mirrored back.

My eyes lock to his reflection. He's bare-chested, his stomach tensed. The bull skull on his torso is heavily shadowed. He tenses his arm and pulls me up until my body is off the bed. Holding me in midair, he starts pumping his hips.

My eyes roll back, fluttering shut.

"No, eyes open," he orders. "Watch your pretty, little cunt get ruined, you filthy whore."

I obey, forcing myself to watch what he's doing to me. I'm heaving, tears sliding down my face. A heavy tremor moves down to my core and I feel an orgasm spark. His cock stretches me and the head strokes against my deepest point, right where I need it to get me over the edge.

"Sir," I gasp out, frantic.

"Yes, Redbird. Use your words."

I'm shaking uncontrollably. "Please, sir, I can't stop—I'm going to come."

He goes still. "Ask permission."

"Please, may I come, sir?" I wail.

His hips go harder, his cock rutting deep inside.

"Come," he says, voice hoarse. "Now."

It's all too much—God, I'm about to shatter in his arms. His grip seizes, cutting off my air. My orgasm rips over the edge, and just as it explodes, he releases my throat. I gasp, the oxygen flooding my body. Making my orgasm soar to new heights, every pulse of pleasure ripping through like a storm.

Wave after wave.

He pumps his hips, jaw set. Eyes glittering behind me.

"Come, redbird," he breathes. "Grip my cock with that pretty cunt, come all over it."

I obey him, down to the letter. Pumping my pussy and feeling every veined inch of his cock as I come around it.

He sinks down on his hands and knees, my body pinned underneath. Instinctively, I arch against him. Seeking his ridged stomach, like steel over my back. He twitches and I catch my breath, waiting for his release.

I know he's close—God, I want it, I need it.

My eyes roll back and flutter shut. This time he doesn't correct me, he's distracted. Hot breath burns the back of my neck as he fucks into my pussy with short, desperate strokes.

My orgasm ebbs and before it can stop, another starts. This time, I hear it. I'm so soaked it's dripping down my thighs. I know his groin is wet from my arousal, I know he loves it.

Sometimes, I remember how dry I was with my first husband. It didn't matter what he did. He never turned me on. But with Gerard, I swear I'm soaked the minute his mouth touches mine.

His hips slam into me. His cock is right up against my cervix, the pressure intense. His thrusts are short and desperate. His hand leaves my throat and he pushes me down, until my cheek is against the bed. From this angle, he's so deep it hurts.

But in the best way—God, he makes me feel like heaven.

His broad body shudders. His breath catches.

"Fuck," he growls. "Take my cum, redbird."

I feel him against my deepest point. He twitches, warmth blossoms.

I didn't take my pill today.

And he's pumping his cum into me. Hard lurches of his body, again and again. Until I'm full.

We both go quiet, breathless. I wince as his cock drags from my battered pussy and he falls onto his back beside me. His hands flip me easily, pulling me into his thick arms. Brushing my sweaty hair from my face.

His lips touch my forehead. His hand is firm on my upper back. My heart pounds. My legs are jelly as I nestle into his chest. Soaking in his warmth.

"Good girl," he soothes. "I'm proud of you."

"Thank you, sir," I whisper.

We lie together for a while. I'm completely spent and ready to fall asleep. He gets up and I simmer in a sleepy haze in the dark room as he moves about in the bathroom. Then he's back, taking the plug out and wiping between my thighs with a warm washcloth. He carries me to the bathroom so I can finish cleaning up. Then he bends me over the sink and rubs lotion over the heated skin of my ass and upper thighs.

He tucks me into bed. I listen while he showers, fighting to keep my eyes open.

Then his warm body is under the sheets. Against mine.

We both sleep soundly through the night.

CHAPTER SIX

GERARD

The next week that passes is bliss. She's off her birth control and all I can think about is the possibility of her being pregnant soon. The possibility of another child with the woman I love. The next stage in building the legacy of Sovereign Mountain Ranch.

I wake early Monday morning, as I always do. The curtains are drawn back and pale, summer sun filters in.

My wife is naked, one knee on the windowsill. Her nose is pressed to the glass. Sunlight dapples her skin and makes her hair glow deep red. My eyes rove over the curve of her spine. Down her tapered waist and the swell of her full hips, dotted with freckles.

"Come here," I say, pushing myself up to sit against the headboard.

She turns, tucking her hands behind her back. A little smile ghosts her lips.

"Why?" she says.

I cock my head. She shakes hers and those brilliant eyes glitter.

"I see you didn't learn anything last night," I say.

She relents, climbing into bed. I bring my hand down on her ass as a reminder not to be a brat. I don't like it, I never have. She gets a window to buck me here and there, but not often. And it always comes with a correction to remind her where we stand.

I pull her into my lap. There's nothing between my hard cock and her bare pussy but the thin sheet.

"What's on the agenda for today?" she says, lifting her hands and stretching like a cat. Pushing her breasts a little closer.

I put my hand between her thighs and part her with my fingers. She's wet, more than usual. Deep inside me, something purrs at the thought she could be ovulating.

"Just you," I say.

She laughs and turns to climb down, but I hold her in place.

"When is your period due?" I ask.

Even after all this time, she still blushes at the question. "A few weeks, maybe more. I can check."

I shake my head. "Judging by how you've been acting, I'd say we should start trying."

"How am I acting?" Her brows arch.

I flip her around and crack my hand across her ass. "Rubbing your pussy on me. Walking around our room naked. You know what you're fucking doing."

Instead of getting shy like she usually does, she hops off the bed and shakes her hair back. Giving me a full view of her breathtaking body as she pads into the bathroom. I hear the shower run and I get up to dress for chores.

For a second, after I've got my clothes, hat, and boots on, I linger on the other side of the door.

Tempted by the faint pomegranate scent of my wife.

But I'm going to be late, so I leave and move down the hall. Cash's door is open and his boots are gone from beneath his bed. I head downstairs and find him on the front porch. Squatted down with his little cowboy hat pushed low over his eyes. He's looking at something on the ground.

I lean over.

"What's that, son?" I ask.

He glances up, shrugging. "It's a bug," he says, leaning back to reveal a black beetle crawling through the dirt. He jumps to his feet and I see him subtly trying to imitate the way I'm standing.

For some reason, I hadn't anticipated he'd idolize me so much. At first, he was his mother's boy, following at her heels. Hiding behind her skirts. But when he hit about four, he decided it was time to grow up. That was when he demanded a hat, boots, and a horse.

"He's your problem now," Keira said sweetly.

Deep down, I always felt I wasn't father material. But that was before Keira, before she'd made me a better man. A braver one. Never in my life have I done something so terrifying as having a child. And she made me strong enough to do that.

I tear myself from my thoughts and kneel down to adjust his shirt. He missed a few buttons getting himself dressed.

"Do you want to ride your own horse today?" I ask.

His eyes light up. "Yeah, I want to ride Silver."

Technically, Silver is an undersized pony, not a horse. I wanted to give Cash a real horse, but Keira was adamant he only have a few feet to fall if he got bucked off. So I went to the auction and found a sturdy, chestnut pony and gave him to Cash for his last birthday.

"You sure?" I ask, rising and heading to the barn.

He trots behind me. "Yeah, I'm not a little kid."

He's so confident. My mind flicks back to my own childhood, remembering how little time I had to just be young. Tragedy aged me before I was a teenager. I don't want that for my son, I want him to grow under my protection until he's strong enough to stand on his own.

Come hell, I'll stop my pain from being passed down.

We enter the barn. Cash stands on his toes to turn the light on. Shadow is already awake, used to being taken out early. I lead him from the stall and let him stand by the mounting block while I retrieve Silver from the back pasture. He's older and has a quiet personality. I don't worry much about him hurting Cash.

I tie the pony and pass my son a brush.

"Get him good and clean," I say. "I don't want to see saddle sores tonight."

He nods, biting his lip to concentrate as he moves the curry comb over Silver's coat. He was in the paddock last night and the dust clings to his hair. It rises in little puffs as Cash works it out.

I brush down and saddle Shadow. He wears a bitless bridle, has for years. At this point, I think he'd take it as an insult if I tried to put a bit in his mouth. I only have him wear a bridle in case I need to secure him, he moves on weight signals alone.

I run my hand down his neck. He's looking a little gray and I know retirement is less than five years off. It'll be hard finding a horse that can replace him.

"Alright," says Cash, setting aside the hoof pick. "Ready."

I nod. "Go get his things."

He drags the saddle, blanket, and bridle out. I hang back, letting him work through it on his own. It takes a while, but he gets it in the end. He's proud of himself, circling Silver with a satisfied expression.

"Go put the brushes away," I tell him.

He gathers them up and ducks into the tack room. While he's gone, I check over his work and tighten his cinch. I don't want to undermine his confidence so I like to wait until he's looking away before I check. He did well this morning. Silver is clean and his saddle is polished.

He saunters back out and I hold my hand out for him to step into and mount up. I pass him the reins and he gives me a bright smile that stops me in my tracks.

Fuck, sometimes I have to shake myself to believe this is real.

I have a family. I have a wife, a son, and maybe another baby on the way soon.

How did I get so lucky?

"What're you looking at, dad?" Cash asks.

I shake my head. "Not much. Let's go, we'll do a loop and check on things before breakfast."

He rides alongside me as we leave the barn. We're heading up the western pasture, right where the Garrison land used to border mine. Before it all became Sovereign Mountain Ranch.

Last night, we ran some young cattle into a separate pasture up the valley. I have some concerns about leaving them that far out, but we don't have another pasture to house them in for another month when we rotate. It's the first time we've used this pasture because it needed to be built back up after years of neglect.

Cash and I are silent as we ride. He's got his hat pulled low, the way I do. He's hard to read, being at an age where all he wants to do is imitate me. Before we had him, I thought it would be easier to see his personality form. But he's so young he's like a mirror. I have to look at the edges to see who he'll be when he becomes a man.

I can tell he's strong-willed, but smart about it. He pushes me, but never too far. And I appreciate that he respects me.

He's soft and loving with his mother. I'm grateful for that too. She's sensitive and it would break her heart to be at odds with anyone in her family.

I glance back at him and see my reflection in his face. Dark hair. Blue eyes. As pale as the early morning sky. I'm no longer the only son of the Sovereign line.

I'm still in disbelief.

My mind drifts back to when I asked Keira to marry me. Well, *asked* is a strong word. Demanded, is more accurate. And she, in her boundless grace, forgave me for my selfishness. I acknowledged then that every good thing I had flowed from my woman.

That still holds true.

She loved me back to life.

My son and I pause at the crest of the hill. The herd is on the far end, a black smear in the distance. The far western side of the pasture is wooded. I know some of them are hiding there in anticipation of the afternoon sun.

"What are we here for?" Cash asks.

Before I can answer, I hear hoofbeats. Jensen Childress moves over the hill on his dappled gray gelding. He stays a few hours' ride from the border of Sovereign Mountain and comes to help on days when my employees can't handle the workload. Mostly in the spring and fall, when the calves come, and when we need to tag and brand.

We wait in silence until he draws near.

Cash waves his hat in greeting. "Hi," he shouts.

41

Jensen looks down at the stubby pony. "You're working hard this morning, little Sovereign."

"Checking the pasture," says Cash, shrugging.

Jensen glances up at me. "I already rode the western border of that pasture. Everything looks good."

"No casualties?"

He shakes his head. "You need to do spot repairs on the fence though."

I glance down at Cash. "You want to do that this morning, son?"

He nods. "I can do it."

I shift and Shadow turns back towards the house. "Keira will be up and Maddie will have breakfast ready soon. We'll go eat and head out in the truck."

We move back down the hill. Jensen and I keep a slow, posting trot so Cash can bring up the rear at a canter. The horses love to run and the ground is smooth and even here. They eat it up quickly.

Keira is on the porch when we pull into the yard. Cash jumps down and fastens Silver to the hitching post. He runs up the path to the house, pausing to say something to his mother before bursting inside. Jensen dismounts and I follow suit, letting our horses loose to graze in the yard while we eat.

"Breakfast is ready," Keira says, shading her eyes.

Jensen tips his hat at her and follows Cash into the house. I take my own hat off so I can bend in and kiss my wife.

She's in a plain cotton sundress. Not dissimilar to the one she wore the first day she came to Sovereign Mountain. I rake my eyes over her soft curves and slide my hand into the dip of her waist. Her head falls back for a second. I bury my face in her neck.

"You smell so fucking good," I murmur.

She shivers. I run my hand lower and grip her ass hard enough I know it stings. I bare my teeth, grazing them down her throat.

A little moan escapes her lips.

"I think you were right about it being a good time to start trying," she whispers.

I kiss her neck and pull back. "Sounds like I have my work cut out for me later."

42

She blushes, tucking her hair back. I spank her lightly, taking her hand, and head into the house.

CHAPTER SEVEN

KEIRA

The week I'm ovulating, Gerard stays close and sends the men out to do the field work. We're careful that no one notices. He comes in for lunch, goes to wash up in our bathroom. I make an excuse about forgetting something and slip up the back staircase.

He folds me in half and fucks me into our bed. My ankles over his shoulders and his cock buried so deep in me I swear I can feel it in my throat.

Getting his cum as deep as he can.

It's a whirlwind and I'm left sore and dazed at the end. Then he goes back out to the ranch and we play the waiting game. Today, I'm upstairs in the nursery taking the linens out. Through the open window comes a soft breeze. The air smells like a thunderstorm. Dark and crackling with anticipation.

Safe in the nursery, I run my fingers over Cash's knit blanket. It's a soft pearly gray and there's a tag with his name embroidered on it. I set it aside, making a note to add a second tag for the next baby's name.

A thrill moves through me.

Thunder rumbles. I inhale the air, tasting a little coolness on it. Through the glass I see my husband on Shadow in the western pasture.

We're alone, Cash is gone for the day. Maddie and her husband went to South Platte for groceries and Cash begged to go too. I know he'll come back high on sugar and sound asleep in the cab of the truck, but I let him go anyway.

The afternoon has been quiet. I prepped dinner for Maddie and set the bread to rise in the hot kitchen. Then I moved barefoot to the nursery to start going through the baby things.

I like privacy for this. Sometimes seeing Cash's little socks and blankets makes me cry.

Today, they only make me hopeful.

Thunder sounds again and I go to the window, pushing it open wider. Gerard turns Shadow and they start moving back towards the yard. He's got Big Dog with him, loping at his heels. Small Dog is shockingly still around, but he sleeps every minute of the day. His entire head and belly are now a silvery white.

"How old is he?" I asked Gerard one day.

He shrugged. "Not sure."

"Well, was he a puppy when you bought him?"

He shook his head. "Didn't buy him. I left the door open a while back and when I came downstairs, there was a dog on my couch."

I gazed at him, still surprised by my husband after all this time. "And you just took him? Did you try to find his owner?"

Gerard shrugged. "No, if he belonged to someone else, he must not have liked living there."

I pull myself from my mind and glance down. My husband is in the yard now, dismounting Shadow. I lean out the window, palms on the sill, and whistle.

He looks up and I feel his slow perusal of my body. Pale eyes burning up my body.

"What are you up to?" I call down.

"Sir," he corrects.

Oh, he's in that kind of mood. I reach up, tugging at the string that holds the bodice of my sundress together. Untying it halfway. Giving him a flash of my cleavage.

"What are you up to...*sir*?" I say, letting my voice drop.

He shakes his head once, jaw working.

"Storm's coming," he says.

"Better get to handling it then, *sir*."

I shiver deliciously—I love teasing him just as much as he hates being teased. But there's nothing he can do right now. He'll need to close up the barn and outbuildings before he can come upstairs.

From below, he gives me a look. The kind that comes with a spanking later. Then he takes Shadow's reins and disappears around the house, heading to the barn.

Thunderstorms aren't common up on Sovereign Mountain, but I've witnessed a handful and they're a treat as long as there's no destruction. Being up on the mountain gives a prime view of lightning for miles. The rain moves over the grass, making it roll like the ocean.

I leave the nursery, moving through the house in my bare feet. When I step out on the porch, the wind whips my loose hair and tears at my skirt. Blowing it up around my thighs.

Carefully, I move down the dusty path and step into the cool barn. Gerard locks Shadow up and pulls the back door shut, securing it against the wind. He turns and his pale eyes fall on me.

Heat moves through me in a wave. God, he looks good. Big, strong, so much taller than me. His t-shirt is stuck to his chest with sweat, his hair windswept. He never cut it as short as I'd wanted at first and now I don't care. I love having just enough length to curl my fingers through when he's between my legs. And I love that his temples are dusted with gray.

My toes curl on the cold concrete.

He takes his hat off and beckons me. I go, shivering when he takes me gently by the throat and kisses my mouth.

"You're beautiful, redbird," he says.

My heart thumps. He's never been an eloquent man. He's never given me a romantic speech or written a poem. But I know how much weight words hold for him. When he says I'm beautiful, he means it.

I run my hand up his chest. Touching the side of his face, scratchy with his beard.

"Should we...go inside?" I whisper.

He glances out of the barn, just as the rain hits the ranch in a torrent. I pull back, shocked by the cold mist coming in. He strides past me and pulls the sliding door shut. For a second, it's dark. Then our eyes adjust to the light coming in from the windows.

Rain batters at the glass. The horses chew softly in the background.

"I think we'll be waiting it out in here," he says.

I'm a little disappointed. Gerard doesn't like having sex in open places. He's jealous and it would piss him off if anyone walked in on us. He keeps the shades down and has me in the privacy of our room most nights. Occasionally, we'll fuck in a field, far out of the way. But never where anyone can see.

"Yes, sir," I sigh, sinking down on a bench by the door.

He crosses the barn, leaning against the window. I'm not going to pout—he doesn't like that and it goes against our agreement. So I wait in silence until he glances over and the corner of his mouth twitches in his version of a smile.

"You're not fooling me, redbird," he says.

I shrug. "I'm not trying to fool you."

He shakes his head once. "You've got that little crease between your brows."

I touch the spot in question and sure enough, I do have a little frown line. I force it away, putting on a casual expression.

"I'm not frowning, sir."

"You are. I know what you want, redbird."

I shake back my hair and fix my eyes through the window. He slaps his thigh once.

"Come here," he says.

He's using the soft version of his commanding tone. The one I like best. I rise and go to him. He turns me around, pulling me back against his body, locking one forearm gently across my chest, right over my collarbones. His chin brushes the top of my hair.

"We don't have many storms up here," he says. "But when we do, it's good for the land."

"I like them," I sigh.

47

"We'll pull in good hay," he says. "So long as it's the only one. Too much rain makes for a bad season."

I think about that as we stand together, swaying lightly. He's so similar to the land he loves so much. He's good at moderation, except for the areas where he isn't. Then he's a full blown storm that soaks the earth. In certain areas, where Cash and I are concerned, he's willing to do anything. He's wild and protective all at once.

But that's why I'm safe. Why I'm not stuck under the thumb of a husband who hates me. Or dead at the hands of my brothers-in-law.

My eyes shift out the window, taking in the torrent of gray rain. Whipping the trees, making the grass roil.

"What are you thinking about?" he asks. "I can feel you're thinking."

I shake my head. "Nothing. I'm just happy."

He rumbles in his chest. "I make you happy?"

"Of course you do," I sigh, letting my head rest against him. "You make me so happy. You, Cash, the ranch, and our next baby. I have everything I've ever wanted."

His lips brush the top of my head. He doesn't have words, but I understand. Instead, his hand snakes around my waist and rests on my lower belly.

"I can't wait," I whisper.

"Neither can I." His voice is low, his breath warm on my hair.

We stand in silence. The rain soaks the ranch until the sheet of gray lightens. Then I see the drops slow until the clouds move on. I smell that fresh scent that reminds me of the garden in spring. The storm has passed.

He pushes the door aside. It groans, rolling back to reveal the ranch house. Washed clean and bathed in pale sunlight.

Then he holds out his hand and I take it. The wet grass soaks my feet as we move slowly to the house. All the fire is out of me. I can wait until later to beg for his closeness. We sit on the porch together. He holds my hand, wrapping his fingers around my fists. Enveloping it in his warmth.

"Cash will be home soon," I say. "I should start on dinner."

He slides his hand around me, lifting me easily into his lap. I push my face against his neck to hide my blush. I love it when he manhandles me.

"Sit with me for a bit, redbird," he says.

He leans back against the side of the house, the bench creaking. I nestle against his chest and release a slow sigh. The air is cooler now. The entire world feels renewed. I close my eyes and listen to the rhythm of his heart and it's different than when we first met.

It's peaceful.

CHAPTER EIGHT

GERARD

TWO MONTHS LATER

It's the hardest time of year before fall comes. We're tagging some cattle. Deciding which ones we'll sell off and which ones we'll keep through the winter. I'm anticipating a good harvest all around so the mood is light even though the work is hard.

I wake early one morning, a little after three. Keira is a lump under the blankets, snoring softly.

Gently, I strip the covers back. She's in a thin, silk slip that reaches the middle of her thighs. With my fingertips, I trace the soft curve of her leg. Enjoying how it dips down and widens. She sighs in her sleep and shifts onto her back.

I kiss the inside of her thigh, right above her cocked knee. She smells sweet, like the lotion she uses, the kind that reminds me of spring flowers. I dart my tongue out and taste her skin.

She tastes like my wife. Like she did from the first time I kissed her, in this bed.

I glance up at her relaxed face. She's beautiful, her mouth full, her pale lashes long. Her brilliant hair spills out over the pillow, tangled waves so soft they're like silk in my fingers. My eyes move down her body, over her full breasts beneath her slip. Over her tapered waist and the gentle swell of her hips.

She gave me permission to do as I like, within reason, while she sleeps. Especially at times of the year when our schedules don't match up. So I part her thighs and push the slip up. Between them is her perfect pussy, a little wet from sleep. I bend and my nose touches the crease of her sex. The scent is sweet and familiar.

I didn't realize before I married her what a difference time makes when it comes to love. At first, loving her was exciting like a storm. Then it was dark and jealous and possessive. Now, it's all of those things, but through it runs a deep vein of contentment.

At some point, our new, wild love became something deeper. Like the difference between fresh rain over the mountain and the cool parts of the river that flow even in high summer.

With each year, the current grows deeper.

Peaceful, like a river.

This morning, I feel a mix of that peaceful love and a storm ready to break through. But she's asleep and I have to be gentle. So I slip one thigh over my shoulder and ease my upper body between her legs. She turns her head to the side, sighs, but stays asleep.

I run my tongue over the seam of her pussy. Her taste blossoms on my tongue. Sweet, a little tart. So addicting that my pulse quickens in response.

I lick her again, pushing my tongue into the softness of her cunt. She moans and her pussy clenches, giving me a little more of her arousal. Mind empty, I lap it clean and push her thighs further apart to spread her wider. Baring her sex so I can run my fingers down the valley and gather her wetness.

51

She moans as I push my middle finger into her cunt. Her hot inner muscles contract. Pulling me in deeper. Her eyes stay shut as I bend and find her clit with my tongue.

I love when she comes in her sleep. It feels different than when she's awake. The build is quicker and the release is wetter.

She moans. I can tell by the timbre that she's still unconscious. Her hand, draped open on the sheet, quivers.

I find her G-spot and work it slowly. Gentle taps, then slow strokes. Just the way she likes it. Her thighs tremble and I glance up to see the muscles of her stomach tighten. My tongue keeps going, my finger strokes her from the inside.

Then she comes. Her body doesn't seize as it does when she's awake. Instead, it quivers and the pleasure rolls through her in a wave. Her hand clenches. She gasps and her eyelids flutter.

Her pussy throbs and wetness slips out around my fingers. Soaking my knuckles and the sheet.

I lick her clean and pull my finger free, shifting up to lay beside her. Those blue eyes are hazy and her smile is sleepy. Her body is relaxed into the bed. I know I can fuck her easily, but I don't. Instead, I brush her hair back and ease her onto her side. My hand moves in slow circles down her back, soothing her to sleep.

"Where...you going?" she mumbles.

"To bring the cattle in," I say, kissing her head. "You rest."

Her eyes flutter shut. My hand moves down to her lower belly, where our next child grows.

She told me last night, as we prepared to sleep. I was stretched out on my back in bed. She slipped out of the bathroom and lifted a test. Flipping it to show the little blue cross.

Then she cried, but it was the good kind of tears. She doesn't cry the bad kind very much anymore.

I fell asleep with her in my arms, thinking about new beginnings. How just when I think I have all that I deserve, she goes and gives me more.

Now, in the early morning, with the sun still below the horizon, I'm awestruck. I can never do for her what she did for me. I was living in a prison of pain and hatred. And she's had the courage to break my ice and love me despite my coldness.

My beloved.

I lean in and kiss between her hip bones, right below her navel. Then I get dressed for the day, pulling on my work clothes and tying my boots. I take up my hat and that's when I feel it.

Hard in my pocket.

Something I've been working on for the last few months.

I pull it out, uncurling my hand to reveal the second wooden foal I've made for her. I smile, in spite of myself. And I leave it on the sheet, in the empty space on my side of the bed.

She'll find it when she wakes.

Then she'll come find me, tears in her eyes.

All the pieces of my heart that she repaired are full as I exit the house and enter the yard. The lights above the barn are on and there's a gathering of men by the stalls. Jensen and Westin wait with their horses, ready to help head up the crew moving the cattle from the western pastures and through the outer yard.

It's the beginning of a new cycle. The weather is already cooling and soon after, snow will come. Keira will give birth in the late winter and our baby will be old enough to crawl on the porch by summer. Then it'll be time to tag and brand and head to auction all over again.

The day is long and it's warm again by the afternoon.

CHAPTER NINE

KEIRA

I got pregnant the first month we tried. I told Gerard when I knew. And I'm four months along when we decide to tell Cash.

My last pregnancy was full of unknowns. This one is quiet waiting. I stand in the doorway of the barn, watching the men bring the cattle in. Cash wants to be involved in everything. Gerard is too busy to take him, he has to manage the entire ranch. But Cash convinces Jensen to let him ride with him some days. He sits proudly before him in the saddle.

My heart stings. Someday, he won't be little anymore. He'll be a man like his father and I'll have to love him enough to let him go.

But for now, I watch him, small on Jensen's horse. And I lean my head on the doorway and feel the first flutters deep inside. It took a while to get used to that during my first pregnancy. Now it feels almost ordinary.

I slide my hand down, pushing the heel of my palm in.

A smile moves over my face. This is the life we've chosen, despite our violent beginning.

And this life is so good.

Sunday night, Gerard comes in streaked with sweat. He washes in the kitchen sink because it's just me in there, cooking. Everyone else rests in their houses, preparing for another week. I'm feeling good this pregnancy,

I haven't had any sickness. Just tiredness and sore joints. I woke this morning with new energy, knowing my second trimester is coming soon.

Gerard wipes his face on a towel and leans back.

"It's Sunday night," I say, glancing up.

He shakes his head. "Not when you're pregnant."

I sigh, but I don't push him. He's right, we should be careful. But I miss the way our sex life was before pregnancy. I know this won't be forever, but I'm feeling disconnected from him when we can't practice our dynamic together.

He moves up behind me, wrapping a hand around my waist. His mouth grazes the back of my neck.

My toes curl.

"You're the mother of my children," he says quietly. "But you will always be my wife first."

I turn, looking up at him. "What does that mean?"

"It means, you're many things to me," he says, in that matter-of-fact way he speaks. "You're the mother of my children, but before that, you're the woman I love. And after that, you're my submissive."

I swallow.

Sometimes it's hard to juggle all the things that we are, but I wouldn't trade it for the world. We keep our dynamic strictly to the bedroom and moments we're alone together and that helps make a distinction. Gerard is a fiercely private person and I'm the only one he allows in. His strong boundaries help separate our dynamic from our lives outside our bedroom doors.

Pregnancy complicates that, but it doesn't erase it.

I know what he's saying. And I appreciate it.

He bends my head back, his hand on my throat. "There are plenty of things I can do to put you in your place, redbird."

I shiver, warmth blossoming.

The water upstairs turns off. I hear Cash singing loudly as he gets dressed and then his feet slap down the stairs.

"Hey, mom," he says, darting around the corner. "What's for dinner?"

Gerard picks him up and sets him on the counter. "Breakfast. I got to choose again."

"Hell, yes," he says.

I gasp. "Cash, do not say that."

He cringes. "Sorry."

I give Gerard a look and he sighs, leaning on the counter. "Don't swear like the men do, alright, son? You can swear when you're older."

Cash nods, twisting his hands. "Sorry, I didn't know."

Gerard ruffles his hair and straightens. "Your mother and I want to talk to you."

Immediately, Cash knows something big is coming. He narrows his pale eyes and they bounce from me to Gerard.

"You're getting a brother or sister," my husband says.

Cash's brows shoot up. He sits there for a moment, the gears in his head working.

"Okay, where are they?" he asks.

I want to speak, but I feel like this is a significant moment for Gerard and Cash. So I stay quiet.

"Your mother is pregnant," Gerard says. "The baby is growing right now, but in the spring, you'll have a sibling. Just like when the cows were born last spring."

This time, it's my brows that shoot to my hairline.

"It's not just like that," I say. "I do not give birth like a cow."

"That's not what I meant," said Gerard. "It's the general idea of it. Anyway, that's all you need to know about it, son."

We both wait, breath bated. I'm worried that Gerard opened a can of worms bringing up the birthing season as a comparison. Cash sits and thinks hard, his brow creased. Then he jumps off the counter and goes to the door.

"Okay, I guess I can wait that long," he says.

I sigh with relief. "Can you go find your chair and set it up on the porch?"

He nods, heading down the hall. The front door slams.

"Do you think he knows about the cows?" I ask, worrying my lower lip. "Like, how the little cows get there?"

"No," Gerard says, shaking his head.

He pulls me to his side and kisses the top of my head. I melt into him, listening to the bacon crackle on the stove.

"I don't want him growing up too fast," I whisper. "He's only going to be my little boy once."

"'I know, redbird," he says.

He goes to set the table up on the porch and I bring the food out. The air is balmy and the chirrup of frogs from the pond is peaceful.

Cash insists on eating on the porch step, his plate in his lap. We're on the bench against the house. Gerard leans back, his knees spread, taking up half the bench. I lean against him, curling up in the bend of his arm.

I see everything laid out before us.

Gerard and I will grow older. Our children will become adults. I see Cash, as tall and big as his father, on a horse like Shadow. And from the corner of my mind's eye, I see a woman with red hair. Riding a painted mare, like the wind.

All the pain of my past broke the day he met me in my first husband's office. It took time and patience to pick up the pieces. But we pushed through and someday our children will be adults without the same burdens, because of what we did.

They'll be free and safe on Sovereign Mountain. In the place that saved us both.

CHAPTER TEN

KEIRA

LATE SPRING

My eyes fix on the lake through the window. At the edge of the water, I see my husband and son, crouched down. Cash pokes at something on the rocks. Probably a shell or a duck feather. He says something to Gerard and laughs, jumping up and throwing it into the water. Probably a rock, then.

There's a sharp little pain below. I glance down at my daughter, wrapped in my arms. She's already got a bad habit of nipping at me with her gums when she nurses. If she keeps this up when her teeth come in, I'll switch her to formula.

I smooth back her tuft of light hair. As far as I can tell, she's a redhead. It's hard to know yet if she's got my eyes or Gerard's. They're still a regular steel gray and from her first moment, they looked out at the world like she couldn't wait to take it on.

She's brave, like her father.

I flip the corner of the blanket. Cash's tag is still there and beside it is a new one I added during my pregnancy. *Luella Angel Sovereign.* We named her for both our mothers, but Gerard just calls her Ella.

He was in love from the first moment the nurse laid her in his hands. In awe, his breath caught. She opened her cloudy eyes and looked right at him, like she'd known him all along. Right then, I saw an entire lifetime between them laid out.

I already know how this was going to go. Cash and Gerard will be close, in sync. Gerard and Ella were going to butt heads and fight until the cows came home, but they'll love each other so dearly.

I wince as Ella bites me again. She starts crying and I lift her upright and pat her back before setting her down.

She squirms, giving me a sharp stare. I bite the inside of my mouth. I know that look.

It's a spitting image of my husband.

I stand and shake my skirt out. Ella lays on the bed, gurgling and trying to sit up. She's four months old tomorrow and she's already ahead of where she should be. She'll be bright and quick. My chest fills with pride as I fasten the front of my sundress and pick up my daughter.

She won't go through the things I did.

Not with Gerard as her father.

Downstairs, we find Maddie in the kitchen. It's Tuesday and she's getting lunch ready before the men come in from the pastures. Tomorrow is auction day and they'll all be gone in the city until Thursday. Gerard, Jensen, and Westin will go with them and I won't see my husband until all the work is done.

At the counter, Maddie chops carrots for pot pies. I set Ella in her swing by the window and give her one of her rubber toys. She turns her head, gazing out at the laundry flapping on the line. Sometimes I hang the sheets to air out because I love the smell of them, fresh from the mountain air.

"Is your husband going to the auction too?" I ask.

She shakes her head. "He pulled a muscle in his back, so he's out for the week."

"Oh, no," I say, frowning. "Is he alright?"

She nods. "But I thought I'd offer to take Ella and little Sovereign tonight, if you want some alone time with your husband."

I can't keep from blushing. She glances up, giving me a mischievous look.

"I remember what it was like to be your age," she says.

My cheeks burn and I grab a knife and start chopping celery. Maddie and I are good enough friends now that she lets me into the kitchen without protest. As long as I respect that it's her workplace, not mine.

"I would like to have some time with Sovereign," I manage. "I haven't just sat and talked with him in a while."

She laughs, shaking her head. "I'm sure you'll talk plenty."

"Maddie!" I whisper, horrified.

She rolls her eyes, brushing back her graying hair. To my surprise, she taps her neck, right at the base. The same place where my discreet collar sits.

"I wasn't born yesterday, honey, I know what that is," she says.

My jaw drops and she starts laughing in earnest. She sets the knife aside and wipes her face with her apron.

"You knew?" I manage.

She can't stop laughing to herself, but mercifully, she changes the subject. We talk about the auction, about Ella, about Cash. About the changing seasons and what the next year will bring. We spend the rest of the morning in the kitchen and I help her serve the pot pies before she heads back to her house.

Upstairs, I lay Ella down for a nap and close the nursery. When I get back to the bedroom, I find my husband washing up. He steps out of the bathroom, shirtless, drying his arms and chest with a towel.

"I want a more discreet collar," I say.

His face doesn't change. "Why?"

"Maddie knows what it is."

He laughs softly, tossing the towel into the dirty laundry. "Maddie doesn't give a fuck what we do in our own time. Neither does anyone else. And no one will bring it up to me."

"Gerard—"

"That's sir to you, redbird," he says gently.

60

With those few words, in his deep voice, my entire body relaxes. He's right, I know he is and I trust him. Nobody cares what we do together when the doors are shut.

This safe world belongs only to us.

He takes a step closer. The sound of his boots flips the submissive switch in my head. My eyes rake over the hard ridges of his abdominal muscles, up over the sightless eyes of the tattooed bull skull. Then he picks me up, wrapping my legs around his waist.

I dig my fingernails into his chest. Giving him a little taste of the pain he likes to dish out. He spills me onto my back on the bed. Then his hands move down and start unfastening his belt.

My toes curl. Oh God, there's nothing like the sound of his belt coming undone. I shift my thighs together—I'm already wet.

His eyes flash. "It's time."

He doesn't need to explain what he means. I already know. We took a break to adjust to our new lives and let me heal. But it's been four months and we've already slept together countless times.

We're both ready.

"Maddie said she'd take the kids tonight," I gasp.

He nods. "I'll take her up on that."

"I'll go let her know."

"No, I want you before we eat," he says, not leaving room for protest.

Before I can reply, he shoves down the front of his pants and his cock is rock hard. Glittering with arousal at the tip. I push myself up on my elbows, but he's over me in second. Hand on my throat, spitting into his other palm. My eyes roll back as he rubs it over my sex. Then he lifts me further up the bed and reaches between us.

Oh God, I'm shattering.

He fills me, slowly. Giving me his cock inch by inch, so I can adjust as it slides into my pussy. My eyes roll back and the only sound that slips from between my lips is a strangled whimper. He growls softly, slamming his hips into me.

"Take it, redbird," he orders.

He draws back and thrusts hard. The bed hits the wall, just as it did the first time he fucked me.

This is what he does to me, this is the place he brings me. One moment, I'm wound tight, and the next I'm limp, riding a wave of thoughtless pleasure.

Bang.

Bang.

Bang.

I can define my life in rhythms. The changing of the seasons. The rotation of the fields. The heavy beat of my bed hitting the wall. Like a train moving down the tracks, steel wheels pounding in a slow drumbeat. Going faster and faster, finally out of the darkness.

We're a swift train heading to a brilliant future. And this time, whatever is ahead, I never have to face it alone.

THE END

Want more Sovereign Mountain books? Westin, the second book in the series, is out September 27th, 2024 and can be preordered now!

OTHER BOOKS BY RAYA MORRIS EDWARDS

The Sovereign Mountain Series

Sovereign
Redbird (an epilogue to Sovereign)

Unreleased

Westin - September 2024
Jack - 2025
Jensen - TBA
Deacon - TBA

The Welsh Kings Trilogy

Paradise Descent
Prince of Ink & Scars (May 2024)

The King of Ice & Steel Trilogy

Captured Light - Lucien & Olivia
Devil I Need: The Sequel to Captured Light
Ice & Steel: The Conclusion to Captured Light & Devil I Need
Lucien & Olivia: A Christmas Short

Captured Standalones (currently in print)

Captured Desire
Captured Light
Captured Solace
Captured Ecstasy

Made in United States
North Haven, CT
06 May 2024

52162489R00050